A Paddling of Ducks

Text © 2010 Marjorie Blain Parker
Illustrations © 2010 Joseph Kelly

Kids Can Press acknowledges the financial support of the
Government of Ontario, through the Ontario Media Development
Corporation's Ontario Book Initiative; the Ontario Arts Council;
the Canada Council for the Arts; and the Government of Canada,
through the BPIDP, for our publishing activity.

Published in Canada by
Kids Can Press Ltd.
29 Birch Avenue
Toronto, ON M4V 1E2

Published in the U.S. by
Kids Can Press Ltd.
2250 Military Road
Tonawanda, NY 14150

www.kidscanpress.com

The artwork in this book was made with oils, acrylic and
the occasional pixel.
The text is set in Baskerville.

Edited by Debbie Rogosin
Designed by Marie Bartholomew
Printed and bound in China

This book is smyth sewn casebound.

CM 10 0 9 8 7 6 5 4 3 2 1

Library and Archives Canada Cataloguing in Publication

Parker, Marjorie Blain, 1960–
          A paddling of ducks : animals in groups from A to Z
written by Marjorie Blain Parker; illustrated by Joseph Kelly.

ISBN 978-1-55337-682-8 (bound)

1. Animals–Nomenclature (Popular)–Juvenile literature.
I. Kelly, Joseph II. Title.

QL49.P36 2010   j590   C2009-903625-8

Kids Can Press is a *l'orus*™ Entertainment company

A Paddling of Ducks
Animals in Groups from A to Z

Marjorie Blain Parker • Joseph Kelly

Kids Can Press

CHARLES HEYER
WAUKESHA ELEMENTARY SCHOOL

Aa

An army of **Ants**.

Bb

A sloth of **Bears.**

Cc

A bask of **Crocodiles**.

Dd

A paddling of **Ducks**.

Ee

A gang of **Elk.**

Ff

A skulk of **Foxes.**

Gg

A band of **Gorillas.**

Hh   A bloat of **Hippos.**

Ii   A colony of **Iguanas.**

Jj

A party of **Jays.**

Kk   A mob of **Kangaroos**.

Ll

A leap of **Leopards**.

Mm

A labor of **Moles.**

Nn A watch of Nightingales.

Oo

A bed of **Oysters**.

Pp An ostentation of **Peacocks.**

Qq

A bevy of **Quail.**

Rr   A crash of **Rhinos.**

Ss

A run of **Salmon**.

Tt

A knot of **Toads.**

Uu

A troop of **Uakaris**.

Vv   A nest of **Vipers**.

Ww   A pack of **Wolves.**

Xx A school of **X-ray Fish.**

Yy A swarm of **Yellow Jackets.**

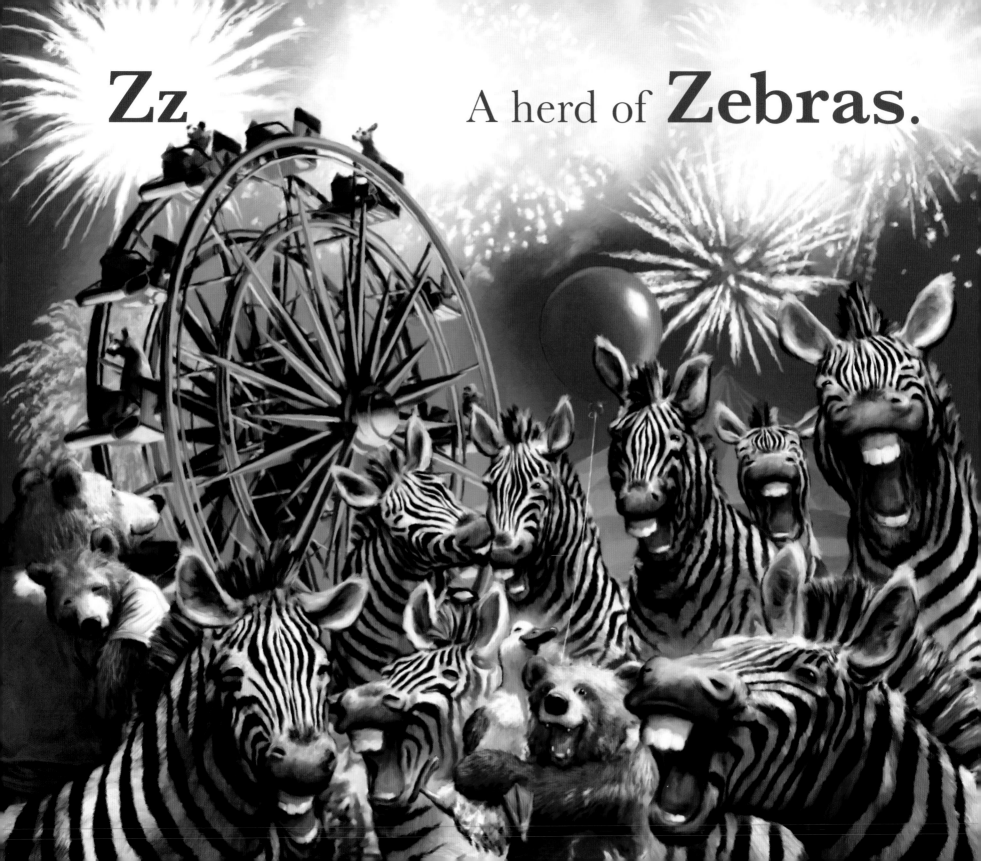

Zz   A herd of **Zebras.**